Subcultures

Carmel Reilly

Australia • Brazil • Japan • Korea • Mexico • Singapore • Spain • United Kingdom • United States

Subcultures

Text: Carmel Reilly
Editor: Ben Haskin
Design: Jennifer Warwick
Series design: James Lowe
Photo researcher: Corrina Tauschke
Production controllers: Lisa Porter and Renee Cusmano
Reprint: Siew Han Ong

Acknowledgements
The author and publisher would like to acknowledge permission to reproduce material from the following sources:
AAP Image/Julian Smith: p. 13; Alamy/Alistair Heap: p. 17; Alamy/Allan Ivy: p. 5 (main); Alamy/David Young-Wolff: pp. 3, 16; Alamy/Eugene Hopkinson: p. 23; Alamy/FAN travelstock: pp. 1, cover; Alamy/Janine Wiedel Photolibrary: back cover; Alamy/Jim Zuckerman: p. 9; Alamy/Rainer Raffalski: p. 19; Alamy/Sally and Richard Greenhill: p. 10; Corbis/Alain Nogues: p. 7; Corbis/Atsuko Tanaka: p. 18; Corbis/Chase Jarvis: p. 12; Corbis/Martin Ruetschi/Keystone: p. 22; Getty Images: pp. 14, 15, 20, 21; iStockphoto/Peeter Viisimaa: p. 4; Masterfile/John Lee: pp. 5 (inset), 11; Photolibrary/Alain Evrard: p. 6; Photolibrary/Stefano Torrione: p. 8.

Every effort has been made to trace and acknowledge copyright. However, if any infringement has occurred, the publishers tender their apologies and invite the copyright holders to contact them.

Fast Forward Independent Texts
Level 13

Text © 2009 Cengage Learning Australia Pty Limited

Copyright Notice
This Work is copyright. No part of this Work may be reproduced, stored in a retrieval system, or transmitted in any form or by any means without prior written permission of the Publisher. Except as permitted under the Copyright Act 1968, for example any fair dealing for the purposes of private study, research, criticism or review, subject to certain limitations. These limitations include: Restricting the copying to a maximum of one chapter or 10% of this book, whichever is greater; Providing an appropriate notice and warning with the copies of the Work disseminated; Taking all reasonable steps to limit access to these copies to people authorised to receive these copies; Ensuring you hold the appropriate Licences issued by the Copyright Agency Limited ("CAL"), supply a remuneration notice to CAL and pay any required fees.

For product information and technology assistance,
in Australia call 1300 790 853;
in New Zealand call 0508 635 766

For permission to use material from this text or product,
please email **aust.permissions@cengage.com**

ISBN 978 0 17 017989 8
ISBN 978 0 17 017897 6 (set)

Cengage Learning Australia
Level 7, 80 Dorcas Street
South Melbourne, Victoria Australia 3205

Cengage Learning New Zealand
Unit 4B Rosedale Office Park
331 Rosedale Road, Albany, North Shore NZ
0632

For learning solutions, visit **cengage.com.au**

Printed in Australia by Ligare Pty Ltd
2 3 4 22 21 20

Subcultures

Carmel Reilly

Contents

CHAPTER 1

What Is a Subculture?

A subculture is a group of people with a different culture from most of the people in their community.

hip-hoppers

Subcultures can be

- **groups of people who like the same things**
- **groups of people who have something special in common**
- **groups of people who have come from the same place, and now live in a new country.**

goths

members of the deaf community

People in a subculture sometimes look and act in a different way from many of the other people in the community they live in.

What Is a Culture?

A culture is the way people live, and the things they believe in.

Language, **customs**, food, ideas and **values** are some of the things that are part of a person's culture.

Chinese people sharing a traditional meal

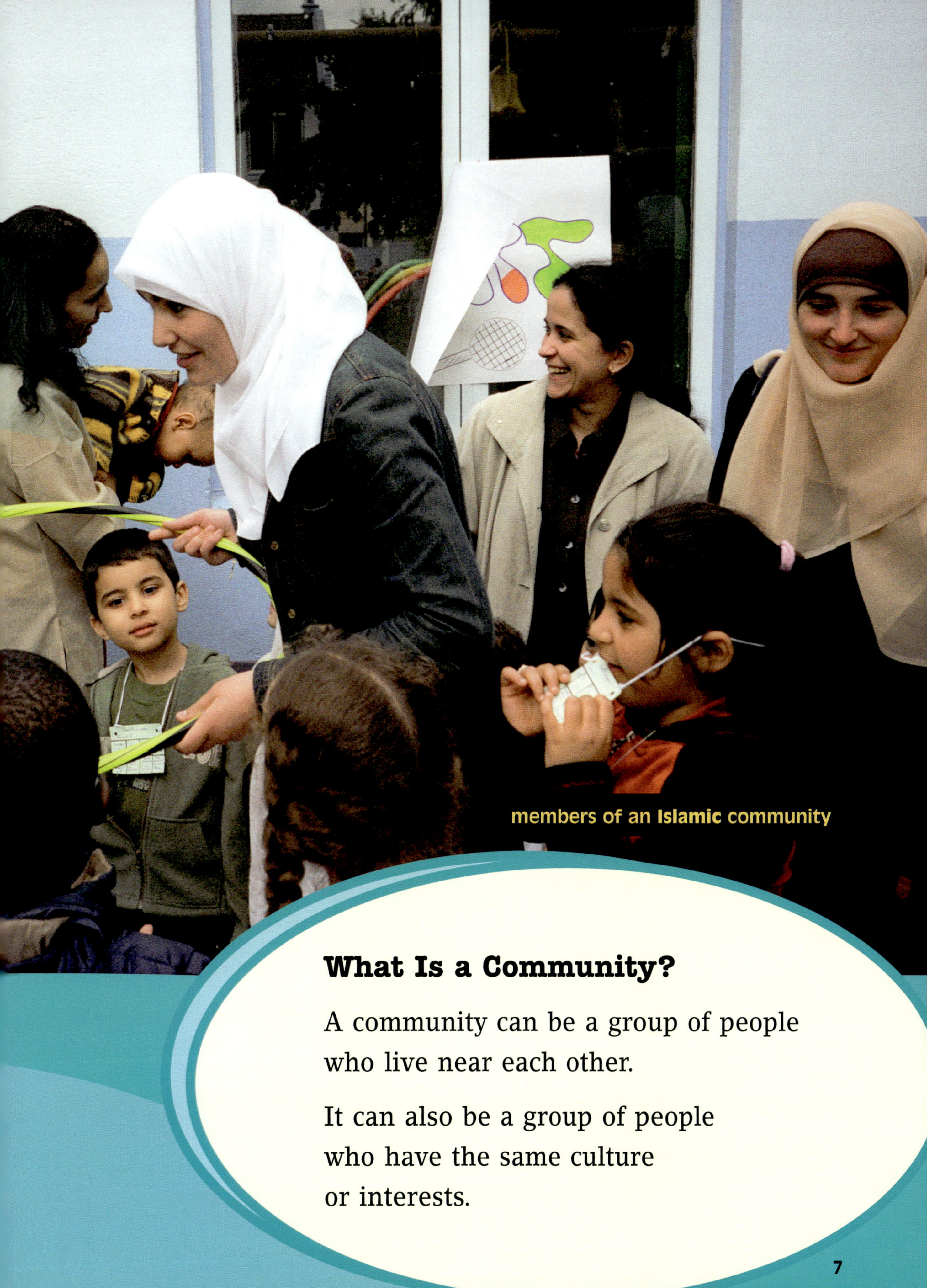

members of an **Islamic** community

What Is a Community?

A community can be a group of people who live near each other.

It can also be a group of people who have the same culture or interests.

CHAPTER 2

Why Are There Subcultures?

There are many reasons why people belong to a subculture.

Hmông people are a subculture in Vietnam.

women from an Indian subculture

Groups from Other Cultures

Some people are born into groups that have a different culture from most of their community.

Many people who have the same language and customs like to spend time with each other.

Something Special in Common

Some people form subcultures with other people who are like them in a special way.

Deaf people cannot always hear a lot of what happens around them.

deaf children using **deaf sign language** to communicate

using deaf sign language

Many deaf people are a part of the deaf community.

Deaf people use their own special language called deaf sign language.

Ideas and Ways of Life

Sometimes, people become part of a subculture because they have the same ideas, or way of life.

Surfers like to spend time at the beach and surf the waves.

Some people care a lot about the environment. They like to grow their own food without using any **chemicals**.

CHAPTER 3

Some Subcultures

Skateboarders

Skateboarders have places where they can skateboard and spend time together.

a skateboarder at a skateboard ramp

Skateboarders talk and dress in their own special way.

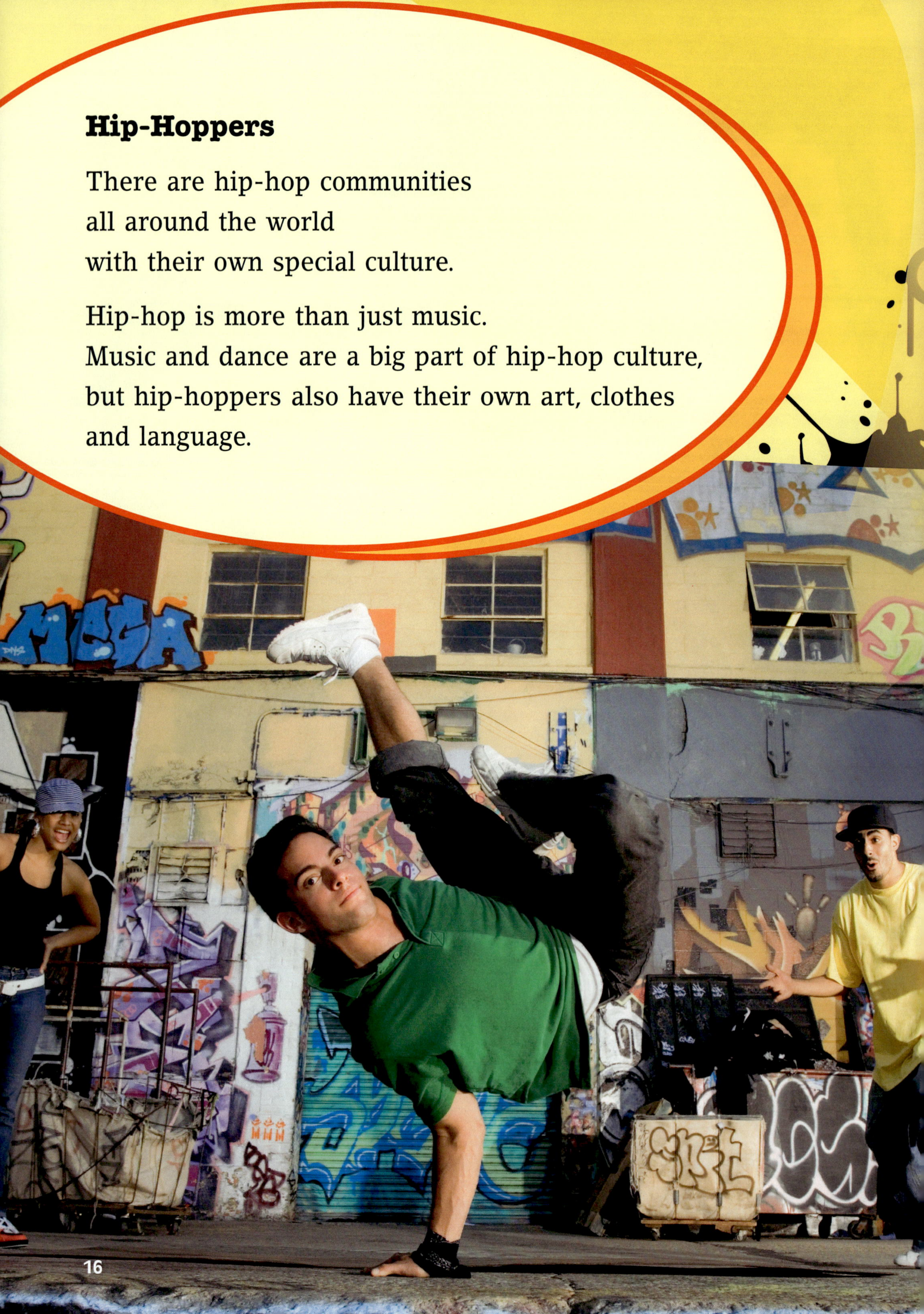

Hip-Hoppers

There are hip-hop communities
all around the world
with their own special culture.

Hip-hop is more than just music.
Music and dance are a big part of hip-hop culture,
but hip-hoppers also have their own art, clothes
and language.

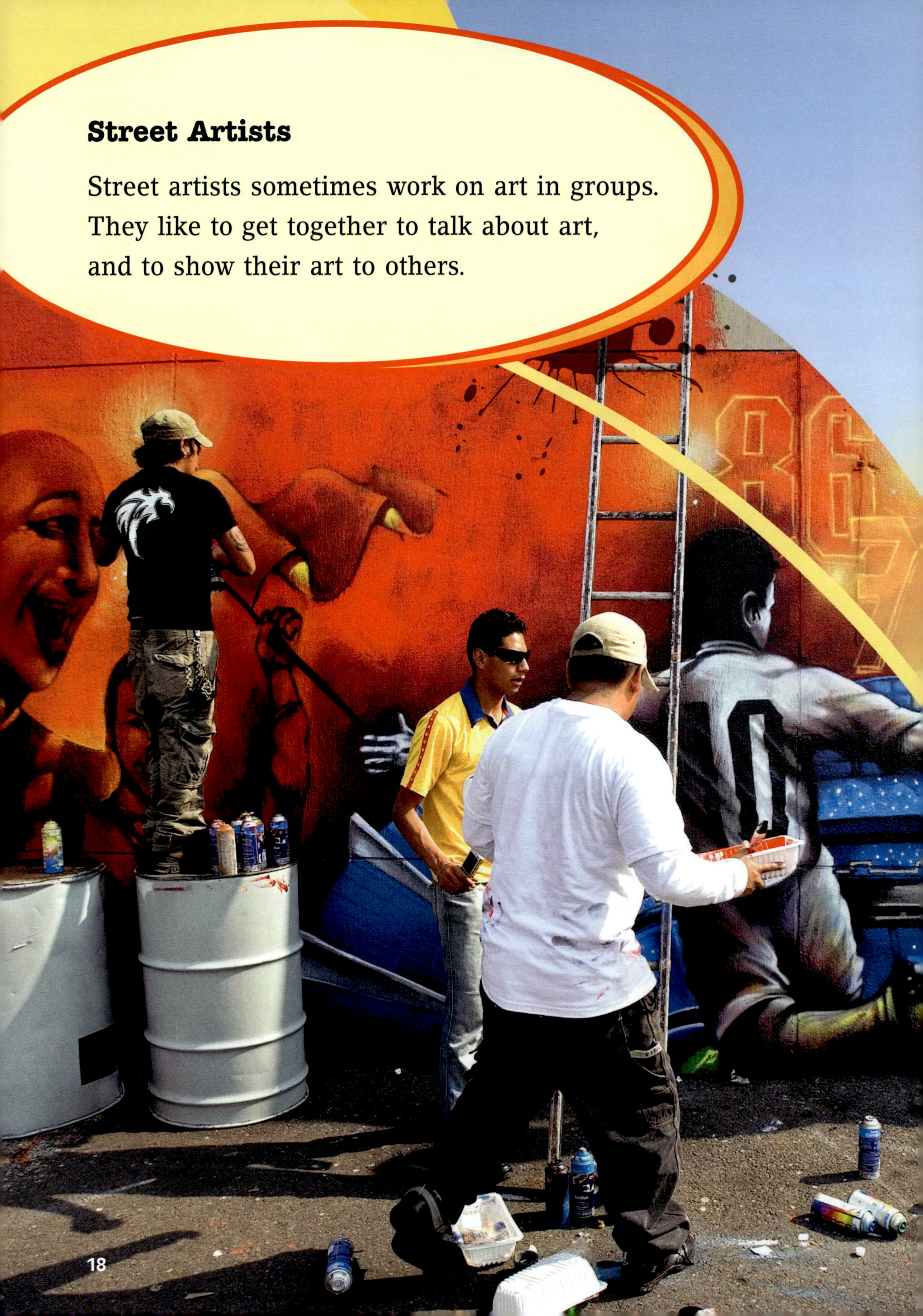

Street Artists

Street artists sometimes work on art in groups. They like to get together to talk about art, and to show their art to others.

street art in Palestine

They believe that art is a good way to share ideas.

Computer Gamers

Computer gamers are part of an **online** community. They play computer games with each other on the Web.

Many computer gamers spend hours
online each day.
They play games together
and talk to each other online.

Being in a Subculture

Being in a subculture helps people
to belong to a group,
and to make good friends.

When people belong to a subculture, it lets others know what kinds of things they like to do.

Glossary

chemicals man-made substances

customs the traditional ways that people do things

deaf sign language a language that uses hand gestures instead of words

goths members of a subculture who wear dark clothes and listen to gloomy music

Islamic to do with the religion Islam and its followers, who are called Muslims

online on the Web

values ideas about ways of behaving and viewing the world

Index